THIS IS IRON MAN

Adapted by Clarissa Wong

Illustrated by Andrea Di Vito *and* Rachelle Rosenberg

Based on the Marvel comic book series The Avengers

MARVEL

Los Angeles
New York

marvelkids.com

Printed in China
First Box Set Edition, April 2015
9 10 8
FAC-025393-20327
ISBN 978-1-4847-2180-3
Not for individual resale

This is Tony Stark.

He owns a company.
It is called Stark Industries.

He makes a lot of money.
Tony is rich.

He has a beach house.

He has an apartment in the city.

He has a fancy car.

He even has a boat!

Tony has good friends.
He works with his friend
Pepper Potts.

Tony has a friend named
James Rhodes.
Tony calls him Rhodey.
Rhodey works for the army.

Tony has a secret, too.

Tony wears a disk
on his chest.
It keeps him alive.

He made the disk himself.

But that's not all.

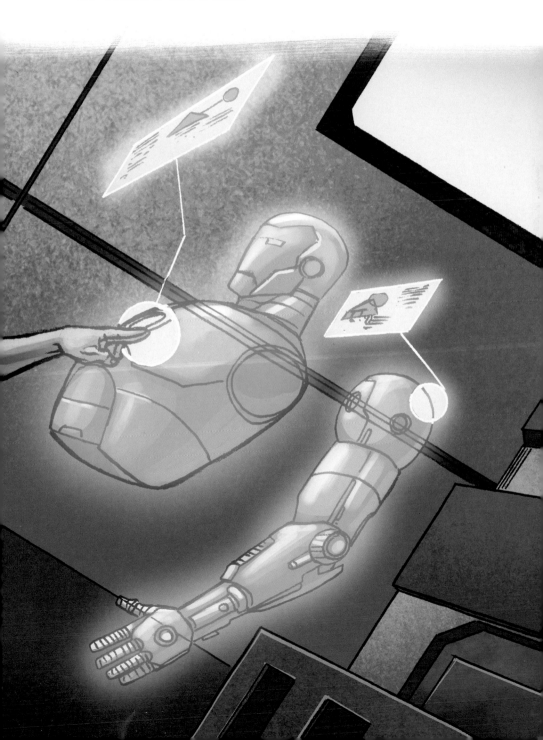

Tony has a bigger secret.
He wears a suit of armor.

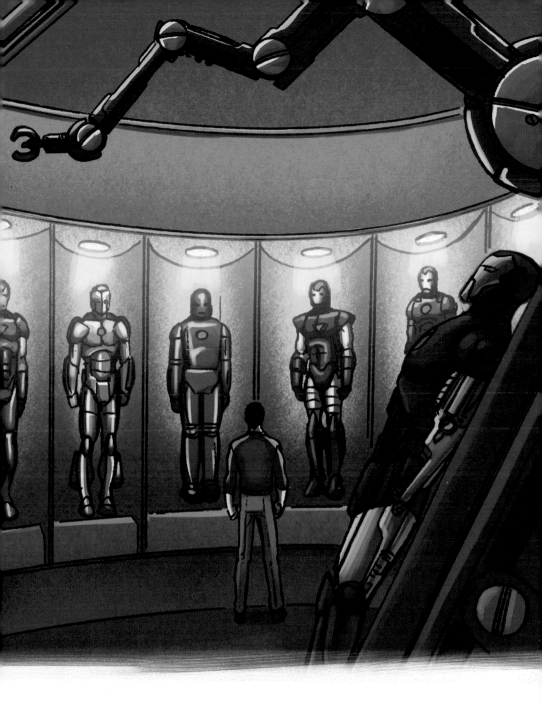

He keeps it in a special place.
He works to make it perfect.

Tony puts on the suit.

Then he puts on his helmet.

This is Tony's big secret.
He is a Super Hero!

This is Iron Man!

Iron Man can fly.

He can shoot repulsor blasts.

He fights villains.

Tony's suit of armor
makes him strong.

It makes him powerful.

It makes him a Super Hero!

Tony keeps working
to make his suit better.

He invents new things.

Sometimes they work.

Sometimes they do not work.

But he is always
the Invincible Iron Man!